# MICHAEL BOND

# A TREASURY OF
# PADDINGTON

*illustrated by* R. W. ALLEY

**HARPER**

*An Imprint of HarperCollinsPublishers*

# TABLE OF CONTENTS

# PADDINGTON

# MICHAEL BOND

# PADDINGTON

*illustrated by* R. W. ALLEY

Mr. and Mrs. Brown first met Paddington on a railway platform. In fact, that was how he came to have such an unusual name for a bear, because Paddington was the name of the station.

The Browns were waiting to meet their daughter, Judy, when Mr. Brown noticed something small and furry near the Left Luggage office. "It looks like a bear," he said.

"A bear?" repeated Mrs. Brown. "In Paddington Station? Don't be silly, Henry. There can't be!"

But Mr. Brown was right. It was sitting on an old leather suitcase marked WANTED ON VOYAGE, and as they drew near, it stood up and politely raised its hat.

"Good afternoon," it said. "May I help you?"

"It's very kind of you," said Mr. Brown, "but as a matter of fact, we were wondering if we could help *you*?"

"You're a very small bear," said Mrs. Brown. "Where are you from?"

The bear looked around carefully before replying.

"Darkest Peru. I'm not really supposed to be here at all. I'm a stowaway."

"You don't mean to say you've come all the way from South
America on your own?" exclaimed Mrs. Brown. "Whatever
did you do for food?"

Unlocking the suitcase, the bear took out an almost empty
glass jar. "I ate marmalade," it said. "Bears like marmalade."

Mrs. Brown looked at the label around the bear's neck.
It said, quite simply,

PLEASE LOOK AFTER THIS BEAR. Thank you.

"Oh, Henry!" she cried. "We can't leave him here all by himself. There's no knowing what might happen to him. Can't he come home and stay with us?"

"Stay with us?" repeated Mr. Brown nervously.

He looked down at the bear. "Er, would you like that?" he asked. "That is," he added hastily, "if you have nothing else planned."

"Oooh, yes," replied the bear. "I would like that very much. I've nowhere to go and everyone seems in such a hurry."

"That settles it," said Mrs. Brown. "Now, you must be thirsty after your journey. Mr. Brown can get you some tea while I go and meet our daughter, Judy."

"But, Mary," said Mr. Brown. "We don't even know its name."

Mrs. Brown thought for a moment. "I know," she said. "We'll call him Paddington—after the station."

"Paddington!" The bear tested it several times to make sure. "It sounds very important."

Mr. Brown tried it out next. "Follow me, Paddington," he said. "I'll take you to the snack bar."

Mr. Brown was as good as his word. Paddington had never seen so many snacks on one tray, and he didn't know which to try first.

He was so hungry and thirsty that he climbed up onto the table to get a better look.

Mr. Brown turned away, pretending he had tea with a bear at Paddington Station every day of his life.

"Henry!" cried Mrs. Brown, when she arrived with Judy. "What *are* you doing to that poor bear?"

Paddington jumped up to raise his hat, and in his haste, he slipped on a strawberry tart, skidded on the cream, and fell over backward into his cup of tea.

"I think we'd better go before anything else happens," said
Mr. Brown.

Judy took hold of Paddington's paw. "Come along," she
said. "We'll take you home, and you can meet Mrs. Bird and
my brother, Jonathan."

Mr. Brown led the way to a waiting taxi. "Number thirty-two Windsor Gardens, please," he said.

The driver stared at Paddington. "Bears is extra," he growled. "Sticky bears is twice as much. And make sure none of it comes off on my interior. It was clean when I set out this morning."

The sun was shining as they drove out of the station, and there were cars and big red buses everywhere. Paddington waved to some people waiting at a bus stop, and several of them waved back. It was all very friendly.

Paddington tapped the taxi driver on his shoulder. "It isn't a bit like Darkest Peru," he announced.

The man jumped at the sound of Paddington's voice. "Cream!" he said bitterly. "Cream and jam all over my coat!" He slid the little window behind him shut.

"Oh dear, Henry," murmured Mrs. Brown. "I wonder if we're doing the right thing?"

Fortunately, before anyone had time to answer, they arrived at Windsor Gardens, and Judy helped Paddington onto the pavement.

"Now you're going to meet Mrs. Bird," she said. "She looks after us. She's a bit fierce at times, but she doesn't really mean it. I'm sure you'll like her."

Paddington felt his knees begin to wobble. "I'm sure I shall, if you say so," he replied. "The thing is, will she like me?"

"Goodness gracious!" exclaimed Mrs. Bird. "What *have* you got there?"

"It's not a what," said Judy. "It's a bear called Paddington, and he's coming to stay with us."

"A bear," said Mrs. Bird, as Paddington raised his hat. "Well, he has good manners, I'll say that for him."

26

"I'm afraid I stepped on a jam tart by mistake," said Paddington.

"I can see that," said Mrs. Bird. "You'd better have a bath before you're very much older. Judy can turn it on for you. I daresay you'll be wanting some marmalade, too!"

"I think she likes you," whispered Judy.

Paddington had never been in a bathroom before. While the water was running, he made himself at home. First of all, he tried writing his new name on the steam on the mirror.

Then he used Mr. Brown's shaving cream to draw a map of Peru on the floor.
It wasn't until a drip landed on his head that he remembered what he was supposed to be doing.

He soon discovered
that getting into a
bath is one thing,
but it's quite
another matter
getting out
again—especially
when it's full of soapy water.

Paddington tried
calling out, "Help!"—
at first in a quiet voice
so as not to disturb
anyone, then very
loudly,

"HELP!

HELP!"

When that didn't
work, he began bailing
the water out with his
hat. But the hat had
several holes in it, and his
map of Peru soon turned
into a sea of foam.

Suddenly Jonathan and Judy burst into the bathroom and
lifted a dripping Paddington onto the floor.

"Thank goodness you're all right!" cried Judy. "We heard
you calling out."

"Fancy making such a mess," said Jonathan admiringly.
"You should have pulled the plug out."

"Oh!" said Paddington. "I never
thought of that."

When Paddington came downstairs, he looked so clean that
no one could possibly be cross with him. His fur was all soft
and silky, his nose gleamed, and his paws had lost all traces of
the jam and cream.

The Browns made room for him in a small armchair, and
Mrs. Bird brought him a pot of tea and a plate of hot
buttered toast and marmalade.

"Now," said Mrs. Brown, "you must tell us all about yourself. I'm sure you must have had lots of adventures."

"I have," said Paddington earnestly. "Things are always happening to me. I'm that sort of a bear." He settled back in the armchair.

"I was brought up by my aunt Lucy in Darkest Peru," he began. "But she had to go into a Home for Retired Bears in Lima." He closed his eyes thoughtfully and a hush fell over the room as everyone waited expectantly.

After a while, when nothing happened, they began to get restless. Mr. Brown tried coughing. Then he reached across and poked Paddington.

"Well, I never," he said. "I do believe he's fast asleep!"

"After all that's happened to him," said Mrs. Brown, "is it any wonder?"

# PADDINGTON

# MICHAEL BOND

# PADDINGTON

## IN THE GARDEN

*illustrated by* R. W. ALLEY

One morning Paddington went out into the garden and began making a list of all the nice things he could think of about being a bear and living with the Browns.

He had a room of his own and a warm bed to sleep in. And he had marmalade for breakfast *every* morning. In Darkest Peru he had only been allowed to have it on Sundays.

The list was soon so long he had nearly run out of paper before he realized he had left out one of the nicest things of all . . .

. . . the garden itself!

Paddington liked the Browns' garden. Apart from the occasional noise from a nearby building site, it was so quiet and peaceful it didn't seem like being in London at all.

But nice gardens don't just happen. They usually require a lot of hard work, and the one at number thirty-two Windsor Gardens was no exception. Mr. Brown had to mow the lawn twice a week, and Mrs. Brown was kept busy weeding the flower beds. There was always something to do. Even Mrs. Bird lent a hand whenever she had a spare moment.

It was Mrs. Bird who first suggested giving Jonathan, Judy, and Paddington each a piece of the garden.

"It will keep certain bears out of mischief," she said meaningly. "And it will be fun for Jonathan and Judy as well."

Mr. Brown agreed it was a very good idea, and he marked out three plots at the far end of the lawn.

Paddington was most excited. "I don't suppose there are many bears who have their own garden!" he exclaimed.

Early the next morning all three set to work.

Judy decided to make a flower bed and Jonathan had his eye on some old paving stones.

Paddington didn't know what to do. In the past he had often found that gardening was much harder than it looked, especially when you only had paws.

In the end, armed with a jar of Mrs. Bird's homemade marmalade, he borrowed Mr. Brown's wheelbarrow and set off to look for ideas.

His first stop was a stall in the market, where he bought a book called *How to Plan Your Garden* by Lionel Trug.

It came complete with a large packet of assorted seeds, and if the picture on the front cover was anything to go by, it was no wonder Mr. Trug looked happy, for he seemed to do most of his planning while lying in a hammock. By the end of the book, without lifting a finger, he was surrounded by blooms.

Paddington decided it was a very good value indeed—especially when the owner of the stall gave him two pence change.

Mr. Trug's book was full of
useful hints and tips.

The first one suggested that
before starting work it was a
good idea to close your eyes
and try to picture what the
garden would look like when
it was finished.

Having walked into a
lamppost by mistake,
Paddington decided to read

another page or two, and there he found a much
better idea. Mr. Trug advised standing back
and looking at the site from a safe distance,
preferably somewhere high up.

Paddington knew just the spot.

By the time Paddington reached the building site near the Browns' house it was the middle of the morning, and the men were all on their tea break.

Placing his jar of marmalade on a wooden platform for safekeeping, he sat on a pile of bricks for a rest while he considered the matter.

There was no one about. . . .

And there was a ladder nearby. . . .

Mr. Trug was quite right. The Browns' garden did look very different from high up. But before he had time to get his breath back, Paddington heard the sound of an engine starting up. He peered through a gap in the boards. As he did so his eyes nearly popped out.

On the ground just below him, a man was emptying a load of concrete on the very spot where he had left his jar of marmalade!

Paddington scrambled back down the ladder as fast as his legs would carry him, reaching the bottom just as the foreman came around a corner.

"Is anything wrong?" asked the man. "You look upset."

"My jar's been buried!" exclaimed Paddington hotly, pointing to the pile of concrete. "It had some of Mrs. Bird's best golden chunks in it, too!"

"I won't ask how your jar got there," said the foreman, turning to Paddington as his men set to work clearing the concrete into small piles, "*or* what you were doing up the ladder."

"I'm glad of that," said Paddington, politely raising his hat.

Suddenly there was a whirring
sound from somewhere overhead, and
to Paddington's surprise the platform
landed at his feet. "My marmalade!"
he exclaimed thankfully.

"Your *marmalade*?" repeated the foreman, staring at the jar. "Did you say marmalade?"

"That's right," said Paddington. "I put it there ready for my elevenses. It must have been taken up by mistake. Now the top's come off!"

It was the foreman's turn to look as though he could hardly believe his eyes.

"That's special quick-drying cement!" he wailed. "It's probably rock-hard already—ruined by a bear's marmalade! No one will give me tuppence for it now!"

"I will," said Paddington eagerly. "I've had an idea!"

Paddington was busy for the rest of the week.

When the builders saw the rock garden he had made, they were most impressed, and the foreman even gave him some plants to finish it off until his seeds started to grow.

"It's National Garden Day on Saturday," he said. "There are some very famous people judging it. I'll spread the word around. You never know your luck."

The foreman was as good as his word, and on Saturday half the neighborhood turned up at number thirty-two Windsor Gardens to see the judges arrive.

Paddington nearly fell over backwards with surprise when he discovered that no less a person than Mr. Lionel Trug himself was leading the procession.

"It's very good of you to get out of your hammock, Mr. Trug!" he exclaimed.

"Er . . . not at all," said Lionel Trug. "My pleasure. I must say, I love your orange stones. Where *did* you find them?"

"I didn't," said Paddington. "I think they found me. Thanks to the builders."

"Congratulations!" said Mr. Trug as he handed Paddington a gold star. "It's good to see a young bear taking up gardening. I hope you will be the first of many."

"Who would have believed it?" said Mr. Brown as the last of the crowd departed.

"You must write and tell Aunt Lucy all about it," said Mrs. Bird. "They'll be very excited in the Home for Retired Bears when they hear the news."

Paddington thought that was a good idea, but he had something to do first.

He wanted to add one more important item to his list of all
the nice things there were about being a bear and living with
the Browns:

HAVING MY OWN ROCK GARDEN!

Then he signed his name and added his special paw print . . .
just to show it was genuine.

# PADDINGTON

# MICHAEL BOND

# PADDINGTON

## AT THE BEACH

*illustrated by* R. W. ALLEY

**N**othing much goes on at the seaside that seagulls don't know about.

So when Paddington went down to the beach early one morning, he soon had company.

"It's a bear," cried seagull number 1,
"and he's digging up our beach!"

"He's made a sand castle,"
said seagull number 2.
    "Look how pleased he is."

77

"Now he's lost his bucket," said seagull number 3.

"I could have told him that would happen. *Screech! Screech!*"

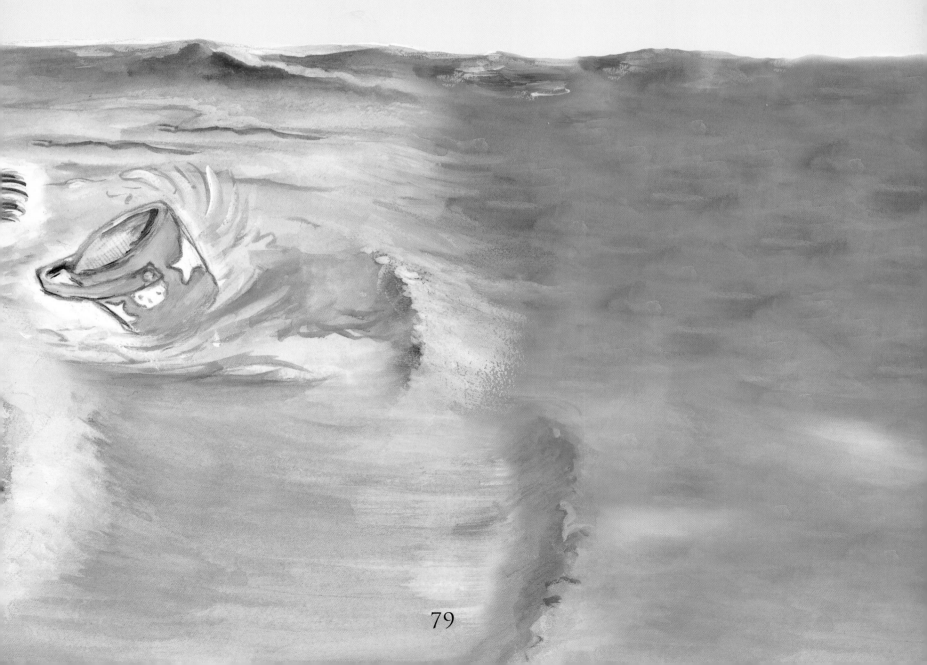

"I think he must be learning to fly,"
said seagull number 4 as Paddington
began playing with his kite.

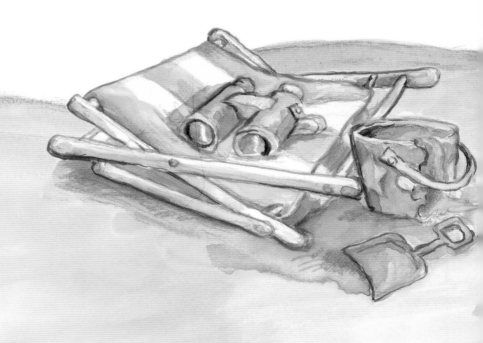

"He's much too heavy for that,"
screeched seagull number 5.

"What did I tell you?" it cried, as
seagull number 6 joined them.

As Paddington was looking out to sea
for his kite, seagull number 7 flew in.
"Look!" it cried.
"He's got a bun in his pocket!"

While Paddington struggled with his deck chair, seagull number 8 landed.

"I'm hungry," it screeched. "Shall I try giving the bun a peck and see what happens?"

"Wait until there are more of us,"
hissed seagull number 9.

Sure enough, a moment later, seagull
number 10 arrived.
"Here goes!" called one at the back.
And they all made a dive.

"Seagulls don't know everything," said Paddington when they had gone.

"I always keep a marmalade sandwich under my hat, just in case!"